Bruce's
Big Fun Day

By Ryan T. Higgins

Disney • HYPERION
Los Angeles   New York

Chapter 1
A Bear and a Mouse

This is Bruce.
Bruce is a bear.

Bruce is a
grumpy bear.

This is Nibbs.
Nibbs is a mouse with a hat.

Nibbs does not want Bruce
to be grumpy.
Nibbs wants Bruce to be happy.

Nibbs plans a BIG FUN DAY
to cheer Bruce up. But Bruce
does not like BIG FUN DAYS.
They make him grumpy.

Chapter 2
The Morning

It is Monday morning.
Bruce does not like mornings.
Bruce does not like Mondays.

"Wake up, Bruce! I made you breakfast in bed," says Nibbs.

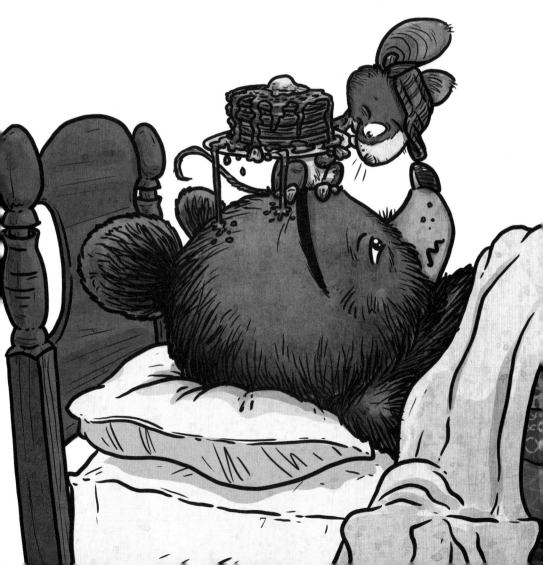

Bruce does not like breakfast in bed.

It is okay.
The rest of the Big Fun Day
is sure to get better.

Next, they go for a walk.

Bruce does not like walks.

"This is a nice spot
for a picnic," says Nibbs.

Bruce does not
like picnics.

Chapter 3
The Afternoon

Bruce and Nibbs go for a boat ride.

Bruce does not like boat rides.

The boat ride is over.

Now it is time for swimming.

Bruce does not like swimming.

Bruce does not
like tire swings.

Bruce does not like
playing in the sand.

Bruce still does not like boat rides.

Chapter 4
The Evening

It is getting late.
It is time to go home.

Will they make it in time for supper?

Yes!

It is a fancy supper.

Bruce does not like fancy suppers.

There is also pie.

"I made the pie myself," says Nibbs.
Bruce does not like this pie.

Chapter 5
Bedtime

Now it is time for bed.

Nibbs wants
Bruce to read
bedtime stories.

Bruce does not like
reading bedtime stories.

The day is over.
It is time to sleep.

It was a day filled with fun!
Bruce does not like fun.
Fun makes Bruce grumpy. . . .

And Bruce likes being grumpy.